HOOF PRINTS ON MY HEART

Autobiography of Junie-B Hawkins

Edited by Roxanne Adams,
Alvera Byard and Caroline Byard

Photos Edited by Caroline Byard
Cover by Caroline Byard

AUTHOR'S NOTE

Since the beginning of "my" time, I have been totally committed to the connection to horses. It wasn't just the awe of their size, their colors, their beauty, or their smell, but all of their God-given attributes that compelled me to nurture their every need.

My first exciting co-conspiracy into "horse-dom" was at the age of twelve.   My dad took me out of school to go look at a racehorse he thought he could afford. This was done with the promise from me, "Don't tell your mother!"   "No problem Dad, my lips are sealed." This adventure blossomed into a lifelong commitment and dedication to this magnificent beast.

This story is dedicated to my husband, Bill, the love of my life for sixty years. He always supported me and the horses in my life regardless of the many fiascos.   -Judy Hawkins

Bill, Judy, Junie-B

"There is something about the outside of a horse,
that is good for the inside of man."

-Winston Churchill

CHAPTER 1

"In the trails of life there are mountains and valleys to cross. Sometimes the trail at the end is best." -Judy Hawkins

My life began in spring on a beautiful farm in Vermont. As soon as my mother licked me dry and I was able to stand, I saw beautiful flowers and fields of grass. My mother showed me how to nurse and her milk was warm and delicious. My parents were Draft Belgian show horses and my master said that I was going to be a show horse, too, so I had to have my tail docked, which meant it had to be cut off. That hurt! My parents were a handsome pair. They were dark sorrel with white manes and tails, four white socks and lots of white feathers. Feathers are long hairs from my knees to my fetlocks, not feathers like a bird. I looked just like my parents.

Those first years were idyllic, racing and kicking up my heels with the other foals in pastures filled with clover, green grass, and beautiful big shade trees.

My master had a teenage daughter who took a fancy to me. For as long as I lived on that farm, I was her favorite horse, maybe because I could make her laugh. Sometimes I would find a big branch and pick it up and toss it into the air, pick it up again, and prance around with it in my mouth, snorting and shaking my head. I would race back to her, drop the branch, and start nuzzling her pockets looking for treats. My favorite was peppermints. She was kind and I loved it when she brushed me. She knew just the best places. She is the one who named me June. Life was good. Master even taught me to pull a fancy wagon, which I did with pride. I learned to go around obstacles and not to shy at spooky things like mailboxes, trash cans and flags. I learned to keep my mind on business. I was even in a parade. Life was so exciting.

Unexpectedly, Master died and everything changed. Master's daughter was in college and her mother in ill health. The farm was to be sold. All of us horses were put on the auction block. Everything I ever knew was gone, including my mother and friends: I missed them.   What would happen to me? I was so frightened.

At the auction, a man bought me. He took me to his home and put me to work in the woods. I had pulled a fancy wagon but had never worked in the woods. It was so different. There were trees, stumps and rocks to avoid. I learned a lot just watching the other horses. After getting caught up on a rock or stump a couple of times, I learned really quickly. My new master was patient with me. I tried very hard to do what he wanted. Some of those trees were huge and heavy. Every day we would go out to the woods and eventually I learned what was expected of me. Master could hitch me to a log and I would go by myself to a yard where his son would unhitch a log and send me back for another.

After a couple of years, something terrible happened. I was standing quietly when suddenly a huge gust of wind made the tree my master was cutting go the wrong way. He was killed instantly and I was badly injured. I still have a bad scar by my eye. It's a miracle I wasn't killed, too, but I was sold again.

Because of my injuries I couldn't do the heavy work I did before. That didn't stop my new master from trying. He was a short-tempered, cruel man.   I suffered much abuse from him. He would put me on cross ties, which meant he tied me with two ropes, one on each side of my head. The ropes were attached to each side of the aisle in the barn. I was unable to move. There was no way to escape. Then he would yell and beat me with a whip until I would bleed.

One day it was raining, the footing was bad, and I was unshod. Master had me hitched to a wagon meant for two horses to pull. As I lunged forward up the hill, the wagon veered to the left and the shaft broke, causing me to fall. I tried to scramble to my feet but was entangled in the harness.

Master was yelling obscenities and whipping me to get up.   I thought I was going to die. I had given my all and done my best. My spirit was broken. Whatever my future held was in the hands of my abusive master. My injuries were severe enough to keep me from doing heavy work ever again.

CHAPTER 2

My next home was a farm in Canada where I had a different job. My new owner wanted me for my urine. Horse urine is collected to make estrogen for women. For mares to make estrogen, they need to be pregnant. Once I became pregnant, I was kept in a stall where I could only stand. A device was attached to me to catch my urine. We were fed well but the workers didn't give us nearly enough to drink. They wanted the urine to be concentrated. There wasn't room to lie down. We didn't get any exercise. We received no grooming and there was only minimal contact with the people. It was a horrible life.

It was six months or more before we would be allowed to go outside again. Usually our babies were   born out in the elements in early spring when it was very cold. Most of them died. Those that lived were taken from us mothers and put into feedlots where they were fed and then sent to places like Japan. In Japan, horses are sold for food. I was heartbroken to lose my babies. I would have been a wonderful mother, just as my mother had been.

I think I was about twenty years old when I had my last foal. It was a difficult delivery. I heard the workers say it would be my last. If I couldn't continue to be pregnant, I had no value to my owner. It was scary not knowing what would happen to me. Horses with no value were often sent to the slaughterhouse. I was in such a depressed state: my future, if any, looked very bleak.

CHAPTER 3

Right before I was scheduled for the slaughterhouse, a kind woman from Maine came to Canada and bought me. She seemed very caring and I was so glad to be given another chance.

That first summer in Maine was nice. I lived outside for the first time in years. I hoped I would never be locked inside again. The lady used me for trail rides, which I liked. The only problem was I had no tail to swish away the black flies, horse flies, and mosquitoes. Those things bite!

The lady had lots of horses that she used all summer and fall. She had a horse day camp; gave riding lessons and trail rides. It was a busy summer, but I wasn't overworked. In the fall she would let people lease her horses for the next six or seven months. They had the use of the horse (a lot of people rode all winter), and she didn't have the expense of caring for them when she couldn't make money. It costs a lot to keep a horse; hay, grain, hoof trimming, dental care and vet bills. Her horses didn't have a barn to stay in; she had three sided, run-in sheds to provide shelter. There was so much snow that winter the shelter in my pasture collapsed. I had no place to go.

For some reason, the lady put a blanket on me. Maybe she thought it would keep me warm. It kept me constantly wet. On top of that, the blanket did not fit well. It rubbed the hair off my shoulders. I developed a fungus called rain rot that was likely caused by wearing a wet blanket. I itched something awful and there weren't any trees or buildings for me to scratch myself on. I was just plain miserable!

The tub that held our water was frozen most of the time, so we had to eat snow. If we were lucky enough to get a little grain, it was just dumped on the ground. Hay was also in short supply. I lost a lot of weight because the other horses intimidated me and I didn't dare to fight for my share of the food. Worst of all, my teeth were so sharp they hurt when I tried to chew my hay. I can't remember if I had ever had my teeth worked on. Horses' teeth keep growing and should be checked yearly to file off sharp edges. That process is called floating.

In February, a handsome black Tennessee Walker joined the three of us in our pasture. The other horses ignored him, so he and I became instant friends. He told me his name was Black and was only going to be there until he was sold. His life had been very different from mine. He had never been abused and only had two other owners in his life. He was young and a very good-looking horse. I knew he wouldn't be here very long and I didn't like to think about him leaving. It was so nice having someone to talk to, and best of all, he wouldn't let the other horses chase me away from the food.

One day in March, the lady took my blanket off. It felt so good to be rid of it, to feel the air on my shoulders instead of that wet, irritating mat. We wondered what was happening because at the same time Black got a good brushing.

Later in the day two women and two twelve-year-old girls came to see Black. One of the women and the girls went straight to Black. They seemed very interested in him. I noticed the other woman looking at me. She was much older and had a kind face. She walked over to me and patted me on my side. I loved it so much I kept trying to get closer to her. She rubbed me some more. I started biting the air and shaking my head, as all horses do when they are being scratched and it feels good and it felt really good. She saw my teeth and remarked that I must be thirty years old.

I think my size was intimidating, because she kept stepping away. But I really hoped she would pat me again, so I kept following her. When she looked at me, I could feel a connection with her and I sensed she felt the same thing. If it had been possible, I would have climbed into her hip pocket.

Please, please don't go, lady. Take me with you. I'll probably die here if I stay much longer.

CHAPTER 4

It was sad to see them leave and, to my surprise, they didn't take Black either. We discussed it between ourselves after they left. Black said it all depended on a Coggins blood test he had to have. The Coggins test is a blood titer test to detect the Equine Infectious Anemia virus or EIA. A horse must have this test in order to go to horse shows or into another state. If the test came back okay, they would come back in three weeks to buy him. I wondered if the older lady would come back with them. I prayed so hard that she would.

Things began to change, I seemed to be getting more to eat, a man came and trimmed my feet, and my owner started putting some medicine for rain rot on my skin. It helped, but I still itched unbearably. Finally, after nearly three weeks, my owner took me into her barn and put me on cross ties. I was so nervous all I could do was paw, sweat, and poop. It brought back all the memories of when I lived with my abusive master so many years earlier.

Pretty soon I heard a truck pull up with a trailer. The same ladies and girls who had been here before, got out of the truck. I heard someone say the ladies had come to get Black. I was frantic! I was going to lose my friend. I couldn't stand still. I knew the older lady didn't like seeing me act up so, but I was scared. One of the girls named Clarissa kept urging the older lady to buy me.

Oh, please, please, lady Judy, please take me home. I'll be good, I promise.

She seemed undecided. She said she wanted to see me ridden. My owner saddled me up, but Judy didn't want to get on. Judy said that there was too much snow on the ground. The only place to ride was on the asphalt road. Even though I knew I was scaring her, I was so nervous I couldn't stand still. That's when my owner got on me and rode me down the hill. A few cars and a truck went by. I didn't shy or anything. Then I was put back in the barn where my owner left me tied with just one cross tie. She gave me a little hay to eat while she and the others went into the house. All I could do was pray. The waiting was unbearable. I didn't know what was going to happen to me.

After what seemed like a very long time, they all came out and my owner took both of us to the trailer. Both of us! I looked at Black. He looked at me. We almost ran into the trailer.

"I don't know where we're going," Black nickered to me, "but it's got to be better than this. Hasta la vista, baby!"

There were two filled hay bags in the trailer. We both thought it couldn't get much better than this.

The ride in the trailer took some time, although not as long as the ride from Canada. When we stopped, we were at a horse farm. When the ladies took Black out, there were several people waiting to welcome him. It looked like a really nice place, and I felt happy for him. When we nickered a farewell to each other, I wondered if we would ever see each other again. I hoped we would; he was a good friend. When the trailer started up again, I had no idea where I was going, but the ride didn't last long. In just a few minutes I felt the trailer slow down as we turned into Judy's driveway. I could hardly wait to see my new home.

Judy's husband, Bill, must have been watching for us because he came right out of the house as soon as the truck and trailer stopped.

"You have got to be kidding!" he said, as he looked at me in the trailer.

What does he mean by that? Will he make me leave if he doesn't like me?

My fears turned out to be unfounded though, because Bill was a very nice man. He helped as Judy unloaded me and walked me around. The place was all grass, no snow, I thought I was in heaven.

Biff, their neighbor across the street, hollered over that

they should call me Lucky. "She must think she won the mega-bucks."

Junie-B looking out of the trailer

CHAPTER 5

Judy and Bill's house was a big white cape and the barn was red. Judy took me into the barn and put me in a box stall and, as I looked around, I saw the water tank. I was so thirsty I drove my head into the water. Was I surprised! It was filled to the brim. As I drank and drank my fill, I thought of my last home where the tank was filled with ice and we had to eat snow and my home in Canada where we were given very small amounts of water to drink.

Judy and Bill's house

When I finished drinking, Judy gave me some grain. When she dumped the can, I immediately put my muzzle to the floor as I had at my previous home. That was when Judy showed me the feeder up on the wall. She will never know how wonderful it was not to have to pick grain out of dirt and snow.

That night Judy left me locked in the barn. It was filled with sweet-smelling hay and water. Even though I was in a box stall, I didn't like being locked in. In the morning, she let me out into the pasture, which already had new grass coming up mixed in with the old. I couldn't believe my good luck!

The red barn

After Judy left for work, I explored my pasture. It had several huge pine trees which were perfect for scratching myself. The land was on a hill with no snow or mud, just grass. The sun was shining. For the first time in at least a year, I didn't have to fight for food… it was wonderful.

Bill came out to work on the big backhoe. I laid down and watched him work and had a nap. It was so peaceful there.

After some time passed, Judy started calling me Junie-B instead of June. Her granddaughter, Rebekah, who lived in Alaska, loved the Junie-B Jones books. When Judy visited her, they would read them together. Maybe that's why Judy and Bill called me Junie-B. I kind of liked that name. It made me feel special. In fact, one of Judy's friends at work made a sign for my stall door with red and blue letters. How cool was that? The days passed and Judy put this foamy stuff for rain rot on my skin every day and brushed and brushed me. It felt wonderful. It wasn't long before new hair started to grow.

Judy was so kind to me that I wouldn't let her out of my sight. I followed her everywhere. Evidently Bill thought I didn't like him, so Judy told him to brush me. I guess I was still wary of men because of some of my past experiences. I soon learned that Bill was definitely my friend. He started   feeding me grain at noon whenever Judy was away at work.

After some time passed, Judy started calling me her baby girl all the time. I guess that kind of makes her my mum. I really like that. I especially like it when she says: "Junie-B, you really make me smile." Oh, some days I'm so happy I could just burst.

Mum noticed how hard it was for me to eat grain because it hurt so badly to chew. Out of frustration I would sweep the grain out of the feeder and it would go all over the stall. She called Jana, the equine dentist.

When Jana checked my teeth, she got very upset. She couldn't believe their condition. I could tell she felt badly for me because she was kind and gentle. Some of my teeth had sharp hooks, which Jana tried to cut off but couldn't. She did manage to file down the sharp edges. They felt so much better. She made an appointment to come when the vet would be there. She needed to use an electric tool to grind my teeth down to where they should be. To have that done, I would have to be sedated. Jana was so kind to us, she didn't even charge Mum for the farm call.

One thing I really had to work on was being good for the farrier. I don't know why I kept yanking my foot away when someone picked up one   of my front feet. Maybe it's because I thought it would cause me terrible pain like it used to after being so badly injured when I lived with my abusive master. He didn't put shoes on me and my feet were in bad shape from trying to pull heavy loads over rocky terrain.

Being so big made it difficult for the farrier, and especially for Mum. One night Mum decided to clean my feet out while I was eating grain. I guess she was determined to hang on even if I tried to yank my foot away. Well, I yanked, but Mum tried to hang on. I literally picked her up off the floor. She landed in a heap beneath my grain feeder. I jumped back and stood looking down at her. *What in the world happened?*

Evidently my feet looked a lot bigger from the floor. I wanted to tell her that I was sorry, but she was very calm and asked me to pick up my foot again. This time I behaved myself.

One day after I had been there for a few weeks, Mum's friend, Brenda, showed up. Sandy and Clarissa also came over. Evidently, Brenda had orders from their friend, Marie, to ride me first. Mum hadn't ridden in almost 25 years. Marie and Mum grew up together and had been friends all their lives. Marie had a horse farm just down the road until she retired and moved to Arizona. She didn't have to worry. I wouldn't have hurt Mum intentionally for anything. When they tried to saddle me, they put me on those dreaded cross ties. Eventually the job got done and we went up into the pasture. Brenda rode me first, then Clarissa, and then Mum. I was a very good girl.

Brenda rode me first

Sandy's Daughter, Clarissa, who urged Mum to buy me, rode me second

Mum's first ride on me

Marie came back for a visit and gave Mum a lesson. Marie tipped a muck bucket upside down and told Mum to get on. Mum said she couldn't, that she needed something taller. Marie told her to just get on. Mum got up on the bucket and tried to get her foot in the stirrup and started laughing. Marie told her to quit laughing and jump.

Boy, is Marie ever bossy! Mum can't help it if she has short legs.

Well, she finally got on. Marie walked in front and told us to follow. We went right down the busy main road with tractor-trailer trucks going by. I could feel Mum getting nervous but I didn't bat an eye at those trucks. Mum relaxed after a while and I brought her home safely.

Since it was hard for Mum to mount me, Sandy brought over a set of six steps that they didn't need any more. All Mum had to do was walk up the steps and climb over my back. It was our very own version of a mounting block.

Mum's six step mounting block

One day when we came back from a ride, Mum asked me to stop by the steps so she could dismount. She took her left foot out of the stirrup and slid down a few inches to the top step. Then she tried to swing her right leg over the back of the saddle and couldn't get her leg up high enough. Of course, the first thing Mum did is start laughing. Luckily for her, Dad was in the garage. She yelled for him to come. He grabbed her right leg and gave her a boost. Then she could get her leg over. If horses could laugh, I would have been in hysterics. She's always calling this place "the funny farm." Maybe things like this two-person dismount that had just happened was why she   said that.

The clump of tall bushes up in the pasture had always been one of my favorite places to go. Sometimes Mum couldn't see me, but I think she could see the bushes swaying when I was scratching myself. She said she was going to buy me a grass skirt since I always seem to be practicing the hula. "Aloha Hoy."

That's not so funny, Mum. You try   going without a tail.

Mum said she should own stock in Avon. She sprayed me with Skin-so-Soft twice a day. It worked better than horse fly spray to keep the bugs away. Those big bottles didn't last long. The Avon lady loved Mum's business.

When the grass started getting tall, Pat, the neighbor next door, told Mum that she could fence in her field if she wanted to. Maybe so that I could have another luscious pasture to eat. That was so nice of Pat. She was a very nice lady and always brought me carrots and apples. While they were talking, I was rubbing my head on a big pine tree. I was wearing a mask to keep the black flies and mosquitoes from biting my head. All of a sudden something started stinging me badly. Somehow, some wasps had gotten inside my mask. I panicked and bolted through the electric fence. I kept galloping and bucking around the field; I was terrified. Mum kept calling to me, but I just wanted whatever was stinging me to stop. I started galloping down Pat's driveway toward the busy main road. Mum's grandson, Chris, saw what was happening and raced across the yard and headed me off. I turned around and went back into Pat's field. Mum got out in front of me and finally got my attention. I let her catch me and she took the fly mask off. I was still snorting and prancing, but she was able to lead me back to the barn and lock me in. She put some soothing ointment on my stings that helped to calm me down and went to repair the fence. When she finished, she let me back out in the pasture and went to buy fence stakes.   In just a few hours, she had Pat's field fenced. I watched her the whole time. I couldn't wait to eat all that grass.

Mum's son, Scott, and daughter-in-law, Judy, lived in the woods behind my pasture. Judy gave me treats, too. If I stood up in Pat's pasture, I could watch all three places to see who was going to bring me a treat first. Life is good! Before I came here, I hadn't had a treat in years.

The next thing was getting my feet trimmed again. Most farriers don't like to work on draft horses because their risk of being injured is much greater than working on a saddle horse. Mum found a farrier who was willing to come and he trimmed my feet. Mum wasn't happy with the job and decided to find someone else the next time.

Fortunately, Mum and Dad knew a man named Nathan. They became friends with his parents while Dad and Nathan's father were in the military. Nathan grew up in Maine and became a farrier. Mum got him to come and he trimmed my feet. I'm ashamed to say I wasn't very nice. I acted badly. For some kind reason, he did tell Mum that he'd come back again. When Mum called me Junie Beatrix Hawkins, I knew she was upset with me. She told me that I was going to be in big trouble if I acted like that again. I vowed to try to be better, honest. Mum used to take care of Nathan when he was little and she didn't want him to get hurt. I didn't want to hurt him either.

During those first weeks with Mum, I learned a lot about her. She talked to me all the time while she was treating the rain rot and brushing me. She would take me for walks while we hunted for the tallest patches of green grass. I knew one thing, I would never go hungry or thirsty here.

CHAPTER 6

Mum told me about some of the extra special horses in her life. When she was twelve years old, her Dad bought a standard bred racehorse named Dew McGregor. She thought he was the most beautiful horse in the whole world and fell instantly in love with him. Unfortunately, Dew didn't do well racing. He toed out so badly that even Mum had to admit that he looked like an egg beater coming down the track. She talked her Dad into keeping him. I guess it was a good thing she was the only girl (she had three brothers). Every time she would get hurt working around him or riding him, her dad would threaten to shoot the #@%$& nag and she would have to turn on the tears so he would cave. I didn't blame her dad though. I would have stomped on him if I'd been around. She got a bad concussion and a broken back from getting thrown off him. In those days, helmets were unheard of. As soon as she healed, she was back riding him.

Mum on first horse, Dew McGregor

Mum's father driving his first racehorse, Dew McGregor

Mum's Mum on Dew McGregor

Mum's friend Barbara Hill on Dew McGregor

Marie on Dew McGregor

Her next was a Shetland pony she named Tam O'Canter, Tammy for short. Tammy came from Springfield, Massachusetts. Mum bought her at an auction and spent more for her than she planned. She had told her dad she would rent a U-Haul trailer to bring a pony home if she bought one. The problem was Mum didn't have any money left, so she put Tammy in the back seat of her Dad's new Pontiac! From what she told me, it was an interesting trip, attracting a lot of attention. When they stopped at a diner in the middle of the night for something to eat, they heard several Navy guys talking. Mum said that they all appeared to be slightly inebriated.

I wonder what inebriated means?

*Trip home from Springfield, MA Mum's mother-in-law Viola, Nancy, Tammy &
Mum*

One of the guys came into the diner and said that he saw a horse in the back seat of a car. None of the others believed him so he bet them that if he were telling the truth, they would have to pay for his meal. One by one they all went out to see if it was true. Then the owner of the diner asked Mum if there was really a horse in her car. Mum said that there was, so he and the waitress went out to see Tammy, too. They were so impressed to see her that the owner went back inside the diner and came back out with sugar cubes for Tammy. She enjoyed the treats and attention. This happened years before Minis became popular. Now it isn't unusual to see them in a car or van. Mum was happy that the guy got a free meal.

At 4:30 am, about an hour from home, Mum saw her dad driving a trailer truck heading for New York for a load. She turned around and caught up with him. He stopped and asked her how many ponies she had in the car. She said, "only one." He was fine with it, but her mother said that she could smell horse in that car until the day they got rid of it!

Well, Mum couldn't exactly stop for a horse restroom break, could she?'

When they were in high school, Mum's brother, Jim, was a good friend with Bill, my new dad. Jim always told Mum she should marry Dad because Dad liked horses, too. Mum and Dad did get married in 1960. That was forty-eight years ago!

Tammy was two years old when they got married. Mum trained her to pull a sulky and she drove her for the next twenty-seven years. Mum's two sons, Scott and John, both learned to ride on her and used to ride her in horse shows. In fact, Mum said that half the kids in Hampden learned to ride on her.

Mum's Cousin Brenda riding Dad's favorite horse, Honey with Mum's son's John and Scott 5 on Tammy

Mum's human son John on Tammy, Blue Ribbon horse show, Rowley, MA

Mum's human son Scott riding Tammy in costume class Rowley, MA 1970

Mum's brother John with Tammy 1959

Brother Jeff on Tammy

When Mum was pregnant with their first son, Scott, Dad joined the Army and they moved to Maryland. Tammy stayed in Maine with Mum's parents. Mum, Dad and Scott lived in Maryland for only ten months before Dad got orders to Panama. They left Panama on Scott's first birthday and moved to Chile, in South America. Mum's friend, Marie, went to Chile and lived with them for a year. Mum was homesick being so far from home and was very happy to have her friend live with them. Dad was gone a lot and Scott was very sick most of the time they lived there. When Dad got orders for Honduras in 1965, Mum was pregnant with John. With Scott's medical problems, they decided Mum should go back to Maine for the remainder of Dad's tour of duty. She and Scott lived with her parents.

Scott's health improved and he learned to ride Tammy when he was three years old. In addition to Tammy, Mum's dad had eight racehorses, all of which proved to be better racers than Dew McGregor. They had a half-mile training track on their farm. Even though Mum was pregnant, she drove and rode horseback right up until John was born.

John was a month old when Dad came home and got out of the Army. They lived in one of Mum's parents' apartments on the farm until February 1968; then Dad joined the Coast Guard and they all moved to Massachusetts. They were able to take Tammy with them.

In 1970, they moved to Cape Cod and lived at Otis Air Force Base. There was a stable on base so they were able to bring Tammy. In 1973, Dad got orders for Ramey Air Force Base in Puerto Rico. Tammy went back to Maine to live on Marie's and John's farm in Eddington. Marie gave riding lessons and Tammy was used for the youngest riders.

While living in Puerto Rico, they bought Trampis, a Paso Fino mare, who was pregnant. Trampis lived at the "Lazy R" ranch, which was on the military base. Mum was worried about the wild dogs that roamed at night and killed foals while the mares were giving birth. She didn't know exactly when Trampis would give birth which is called foaling. So Mum waited eighteen nights with Trampis in a special pasture at the ranch until it was Trampis' time to foal. That happened on May 14, 1974, and Mum helped Trampis bring her foal into the world. The foal would have died if Mum hadn't been there. The birth sack was drawn so tight over his face he couldn't breathe. But Mum knew just what to do. She pulled the sack away and cleared out his nostrils; another life saved by my Mum!

Trampis with foal 9 hours old

Scott and John helped pick out a name for the foal. Since he was born just after midnight, they decided to call him Stardust . . . Dusty for short. He had a white star on his forehead and was black. He turned gray as he grew older. He was such a fun horse to ride. Paso Finos are known for being the smoothest riding horses in the world. They have a one, two, three, four beat to their stride. The rider remains virtually motionless, no bouncing, like you do when you're trotting on other breeds. The Puerto Ricans demonstrate their smooth gaits by riding with a glass of wine on top of their hats. About the same time that they bought Trampis,

Mum and Dad found another mare, Negra, for Scott to ride. She was much more spirited and a good match for Scott. John liked Trampis the best.

Dad and Dusty and Trampis

Mum's human son Scott on Negra, November 23,1974

Mum's human son John on Negra, February 15, 1975

CHAPTER 7

Mum worked at the lunch counter at the ranch. Dad used to trim the feet of the horses at the ranch. There were 120 horses in the herd and he did a lot of them. One day he came into the ranch's clubhouse to get a cold drink and said to Mum "You should see the tall skinny horse across the road."

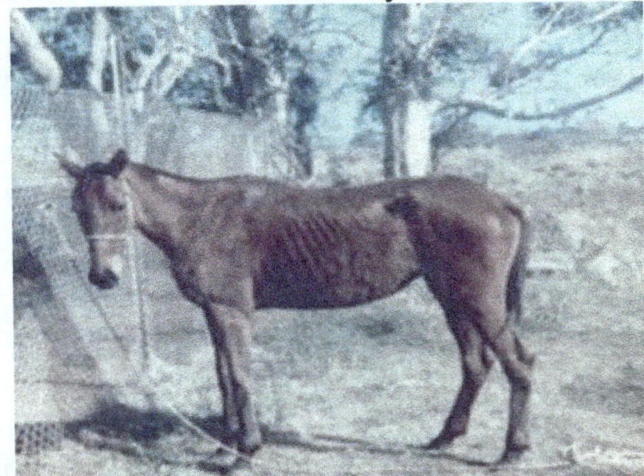
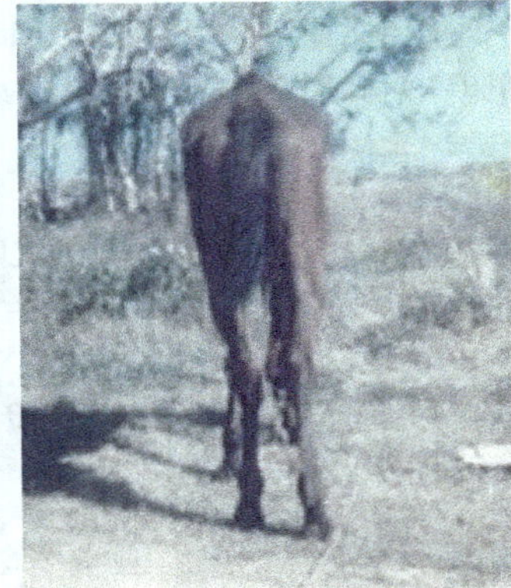

Twiggy, February 10, 1975

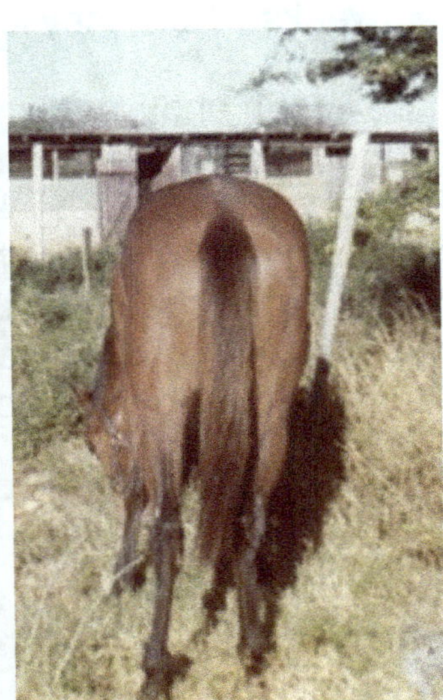

Twiggy, one year later, February 1976

Honestly, wouldn't you think he should have known better than say that to her?

Anyway, she asked Dad to watch the counter while she went to look at the horse. The horse was a thoroughbred and only about 2 1/2 years old. Mum said she was the skinniest horse she had ever seen. She had blood running out of both nostrils and down both legs where she kept kicking herself. She could barely stand. To make a long story short, Mum bought her for twenty-five dollars and a bag of grain. She named her Twiggy for obvious reasons. The next morning when she and Dad went out to feed her, Mum called to her. She nickered. She went over to Mum and held her head against her chest. Well, I guess you know Mum melted and told Twiggy, "Don't you worry; Mama will take care of you."

Dad said, "Don't get any ideas, we aren't taking horses back to the states!" Mum said, "I know that."

I think Mum had a plan even then. Dad is such a sucker.

John and Debbie were good friends of Mum and Dad. They all arrived in Puerto Rico at the same time and lived across the street from each other. In fact, their son Nathan was born just two weeks before they left Cape Cod. Nathan is now my farrier.

John and Debbie went back to Cape Cod after two years in Puerto Rico. When they left they shipped their pregnant Paso Fino mare, Downy, back, too. When it was time for Mum, Dad, and the boys to be transferred back to Cape Cod the following year, John suggested Mum and Dad ship their horses to Florida and he would drive to Florida and pick them up. But John wanted Mum and Dad to find another mare for him and Debbie.

Mum on Twiggy, 1976

Dad on Negra

I wonder what changed Dad's mind about shipping horses. As if I didn't know? Dad says Mum is softer than a sneaker full of you know what. She's not the only one.

Mum and Dad started looking for a mare for John and Debbie and found one just one day before the horses had to go into quarantine. Her name was Star and she was covered with ticks. So, Mum and Dad got to spend their sixteenth anniversary, March 24, 1976, picking ticks off Star until 1:00 am the following morning. Before they went home for a little sleep, they mixed corral and mineral oil together and completely soaked her down. Mum's mom and stepfather were visiting and even her mom went back to the stable at five in the morning to help pick ticks off Star. Mum said you could wiggle your fingers in her mane and tail and the ticks would fall like grapes. Mum thought that there could be a problem shipping Twiggy or Star since they were so infested with ticks, but it was Dusty who had to be treated. He tolerated the drugs well, much to everyone's relief.

Mum's mother "Bessie" picking ticks off Star

After the blood was drawn, the tick inspector would completely soak the horses down with an insecticide. For tick control, there had to be a six-foot grass-free area away from the horse stalls. If the tick inspector found a live tick on any horse on the day you shipped, that horse was not allowed to go.

Evidently shipping horses isn't as easy as one might think. Phone service on the island was very poor. It was very stressful trying to coordinate the USDA veterinarian and the tick inspector to be there at the same time; but they arrived as scheduled and blood was drawn on each horse. The tests had to be sent away to see if they had piroplasmosis, a disease caused by ticks. If they had it, they could be treated, but you had to sign a release because the treatment could cause death. Two other people were shipping their horses at the same time. That made a total of eleven horses being tested. Everyone had to wait with bated breath for test results.

As the weeks went by, the horses were getting antsier by the day. They were used to being outside all the time, not in a stall. Dusty, being a mischievous two-year old, kept getting into trouble. One night he managed to take the plug out of his water trough and turn the water on full blast. By morning the water had flooded three other stalls: he wasn't very popular. Mum and Dad weren't happy, either. They had to use sand in the stalls because no bedding was allowed. They had to go get a couple of truckloads of sand and replace all four stalls.

The four-foot high walls of the stalls were made of concrete blocks. Because of the heat, the tops of the walls were made of chain link fencing. Every stall had a huge wall locker for supplies. One morning, Mum drove to the stable to find Dusty looking like he had grown two feet taller. Somehow he had managed to tip over the wall locker and was standing on top of it! It's a wonder he didn't hurt himself! It was a lot of work.

Boy, talk about stress!!

Shortly after the horses went into quarantine, Mum's Mom and stepfather left Puerto Rico to visit Mum's stepsister in Florida. While there, they found a used horse trailer and bought it for Mum and Dad so they wouldn't have that job to do once they arrived in Florida. Mum's stepsister found a place to board the horses while waiting for

John to drive down from Cape Cod. She also found a woman to drive ninety miles to Miami to be there when the plane landed. If no one was there when the plane landed, the horses would have to be put into stalls near the airport at a cost of one hundred dollars per horse per day; and that price applied even if the horses were there for only an hour.

Wait a minute, did Mum say plane? No way, horses can't fly in a plane. Can they? I'd be scared to death. I guess if it was the only way to be with Mum, I'd do it.

With the phone service so bad it was hard trying to reach the guys that shipped cattle to Puerto Rico from Miami. They would ship horses back to Miami for a hundred dollars each, which was a great deal. Because Twiggy was a thoroughbred, they said he would have to be in a stall and be the first one on the plane. Thoroughbreds are much higher strung than Paso Finos. They also told Mum and Dad that if she started thrashing around, they would have no other choice but to shoot her as she could cause the plane to crash. That was a scary thought. Twiggy was getting twenty pounds of grain a day, was very young, and a bundle of energy.

Mum said she would listen at night for the sound of the plane. She was so afraid that something would go wrong. They finally got word that a load of cattle would be landing early one morning in the middle of May. Mum finally got through to her stepsister in Florida to contact the lady who would meet the plane. It was so important that she be there before noon. Then she had to reach the USDA veterinarian and the tick inspector. They couldn't leave the quarantine stalls before they were inspected for ticks and given the proper paperwork.

As soon as Mum got the "thumbs up" she tranquilized all three horses and Dad led Twiggy, Mum led Dusty, and Scott led Star. It was a half-mile walk to the plane. One of the other people shipping horses had made a ramp for the horses to go up. The cattle were unloaded onto a large truck that had a high body. The plane ramp didn't reach the ground. Unfortunately, when the extension ramp was built, the bottom half of the ramp was left open. Had Dad known earlier, it could have been fixed. Twiggy had to be loaded first because the stall for her was up near the front of the plane. Twiggy wanted no part of that. It was a very long steep ramp and must have been very scary for all the horses. Finally, Mum had to give her more tranquilizers. Still no luck. Somebody suggested blindfolding her, which Mum finally tried. Twiggy started up the ramp and then she collapsed spread- eagled with her hind legs on each side of the ramp. The men had to tear the ramp apart to free her. Mum was in tears. But Twiggy was able to stand. Nothing appeared to be broken, but the insides of her legs looked like raw hamburg.

Mum and Dad went out to the Lazy R Clubhouse to find some lumber to rebuild the ramp. When they got back, someone had backed a horse trailer up to what was left of the ramp. The plane crew had taken apart the metal rail pens and put them along side the ramp. Dad got Twiggy in the trailer and headed up the ramp. This time she followed Dad all the way up and went in. Everyone was cheering except Mum who was crying with relief. She knew if Twiggy wouldn't load, then they would have to leave her behind.

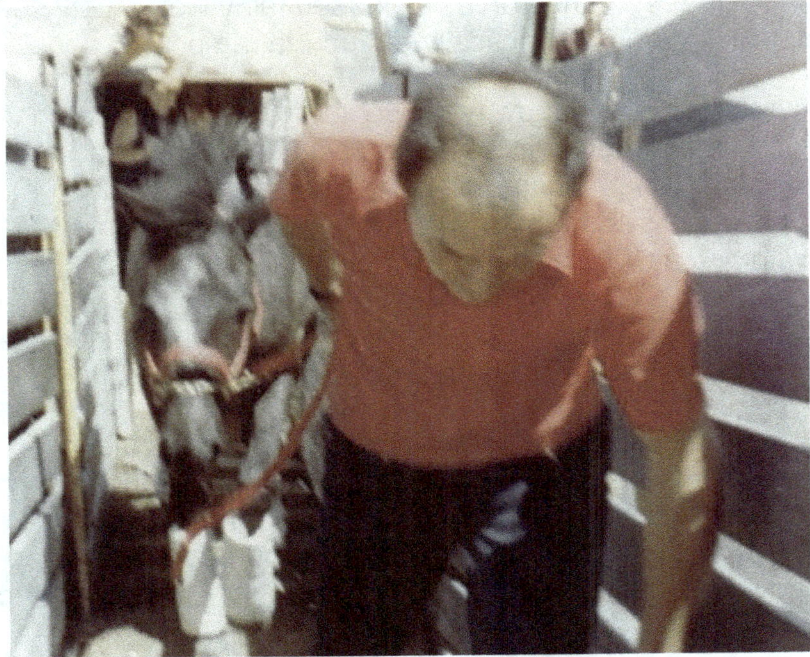

Dad leading Dusty on the plane

Loading Horses on plane

The rest of the horses all loaded fairly well. Dusty seemed eager to get on and practically ran up the ramp.

The pilot and crew were wonderful so patient and helpful. Twiggy had put them hours behind schedule. They had planned on coming back the same day with another load of cattle. Dad had planned to come back with them. Instead he wanted Mum to go with him as Twiggy definitely needed to be seen by a veterinarian and would need someone to care for her. There wasn't any way to contact the lady who was supposed to meet the plane that they were going to be several hours late.

On the flight to Miami there was a lot of turbulence. Several of the horses fell down. Mum said that Dusty appeared to be the only one enjoying the adventure. Mum had to move him twice because he kept untying the other horses. Dad stayed with Twiggy. They were thankful Twiggy had a stall as it was much safer for her.

Mum and Dad, were so grateful the lady had waited for

hours for the plane to arrive. It was very late when they reached West Palm Beach with the horses. They got the horses settled in for the night and then Mum and Dad went to her step-sister's house. It had been a very long day.

They called the veterinarian the next morning. He told Mum what to do for the next week. By then Twiggy no longer needed shots of medication, just rest. The movers were supposed to be at their home in Puerto Rico in a couple of days and Mum and Dad needed to be there. They had to fly back to Puerto Rico on a commercial airline. That was an added expense they didn't need.

Mum's Cousin Tami on Twiggy in Puerto Rico

CHAPTER 8

A week later Mum put Scott and John on a plane for Maine. Mum flew to Miami. Dad had to stay several weeks longer in Puerto Rico. John and a friend of his, Mike, picked Mum up at the airport. John's mother lived in Miami so they had a place to stay.

The next morning Mum, John, and Mike drove up to West Palm Beach to see the horses and to pick up the horse trailer. John had to check the trailer to make sure it was road ready. While they were there, a girl talked to Mum and said that she would like to buy Twiggy. Mum told her that she wasn't for sale. Then she asked if she could ride her. Mum told her she had been injured and wouldn't be able to be ridden for quite a while.

The next morning Mum's step-sister called and told her Twiggy was down in her stall and couldn't get up. She offered to meet Mum half-way to Miami so John and Mike took her up to meet her. The vet arrived right after they got to the stable. Twiggy's upper leg was horribly swollen and she was in a lot of pain. It was obvious that she had been ridden and probably jumped. The vet told Mum to give her antibiotics in her jugular vein and pain shots intramuscular for ten days. He also told her to soak her hind leg and hip for a half-hour of heat and a half-hour of cold as long as she could. Then bandage her lower legs and head for Cape Cod. For the next eighteen hours Mum never left Twiggy. She did the cold and hot soaks for that long.

A couple of days later Mum called John and told them she was ready to go. The horse trailer was ready so they came the following morning to pick up the horses. Dusty, being the smallest, had to ride backwards in the dressing room all the way to Cape Cod.

The first stop heading north was a rest area on the interstate in Jessup, Georgia. The first thing they did was unload the horses out of the trailer for some exercise. Then they tied them to the trailer while they ate a picnic supper. Without warning, something startled Twiggy and she broke her lead rope and was loose. Because of her leg injuries she wasn't able to run, which turned out to be a blessing.   Mum was able to catch her before she got out onto the interstate. When it was time to load them back into the trailer, Twiggy and Star decided that they had had enough riding for one day. Dusty was eager to get going and jumped right back into the dressing room. Evidently, he enjoyed riding backwards. It was starting to get dark when Twiggy finally decided to cooperate and got in. It was pitch dark and all they had for a light was a flashlight. Finally, Star got into the trailer. After that exhausting experience, John announced that they weren't letting them out again until they reached Cape Cod!

Mum giving Twiggy shot on the trip to Cape Cod from Miami, FL

John taking a break on trip from Miami to Cape Cod.

Rest stop on the way to Cape Cod from Florida, May 1976, John and Mike

They spent two nights on the road. Mum stayed in the truck to be near the horses. Twiggy was nervous and a wind sucker, which meant she would bob her head up and down and then take a gulp of air. This would make the truck shake so much that Mum didn't get much sleep. Most horses have to bite on something and then swallow. Evidently it releases endorphins in their brains and makes them feel good. It's a very bad habit and if horses are confined to a stall much of the time and one horse starts doing this, other horses will pick up the habit. It makes it hard to keep weight on a horse that does this.

The second morning they were in Maryland. They stopped at a McDonalds for breakfast. Evidently, they were very close to a racetrack. Mum was giving Twiggy her shots when someone blew a trumpet that calls the horses at the start of a race. Twiggy started getting very excited. Mum figured that Twiggy thought she was in a starting gate instead of a trailer. They left that parking lot in a hurry!

The rest of the trip was just long. It was the middle of the night when they finally reached Otis AFB on Cape Cod. Downy, the horse that John and Debbie had brought home from Puerto Rico the year before, had twin foals while they were on their way home. Mum said they were the cutest foals she had ever seen.

Debbie with Tiny Tim & Mighty Mac. The mother is Downy, the mare they brought back from the Puerto Rico.

Downy with twin foals

Mum stayed with John and Debbie for a couple of days until her cousin, Tami, and her boyfriend, Wayne, came down from Maine with Mum's truck to take them home.

Mum had been back in Maine only a couple of days when Dad's father had a heart attack. Dad was still in Puerto Rico and he had to come home several weeks early. Thankfully his father survived and was back home after three weeks in the hospital.

CHAPTER 9

It was a tough summer for Mum and Dad and their families. Three weeks after Dad's father had his heart attack, Mum's step-father spent six weeks in the hospital before he passed away. Just before he died, Dad was riding his motorcycle back to Cape Cod. He made it all the way to the base and had an accident. His leg was badly crushed. He had to go by ambulance to a hospital in Boston. The next day Mum and John loaded Twiggy, Dusty, and Mum's Shetland pony, Tammy (Marie had been taking care of Tammy for the previous three years), into the trailer to go back to Cape Cod. They also had rescued a dog named Cricket from a shelter. She went with them. Since it was the middle of August and hot, Mum decided to wait until evening to leave. She was about a hundred miles from her mother's house when the truck and trailer lights went out. Scott had to shine a flashlight out the window so Mum could drive in the breakdown lane until she reached the next rest area. She said it was scary when trailer trucks went by. She was afraid they would get hit. They spent the night at the rest area and when it was daylight they continued on to the Cape.

Mum picked Dad up a couple of days later. He had a cast on his leg from his foot to his hip for several months. They had been home two days when Mum's step-father passed away. Mum's brother John lived in Connecticut and owned a station wagon, so he came to the Cape and picked up Mum, Dad, Scott and John for the trip back to Maine for the funeral. Dad had to keep his leg elevated as much as possible. It pained him a lot.

They lived at Otis Air Force Base for the next four years until Dad retired from the Coast Guard in 1980. They moved back to Maine and settled in Eddington, just a mile from John and Marie's horse farm. Mum gave Twiggy to Marie who trained her in dressage and also raised a couple of foals from her. Scott no longer rode and she was too much horse for Mum to ride. She and John liked to ride Dusty and they both drove Tammy. Tammy was twenty-eight years old when she died in 1986. Mum was heartbroken.

Dusty got sick on Mum's and Dad's forty-third wedding anniversary. They couldn't get a vet to come and he was in so much pain, Dad had to put him down. That was an incredibly sad day. Dusty had been part of the family for nearly twenty-nine years. She still had Rocky. Rocky was a thirty-one-inch miniature stallion. Mum's brother, Jim, and sister-in-law, Betty, raised miniature horses and gave Rocky to Mum. Mum used to show him a lot. Dad used to call Rocky the "sidewalk superintendent" as he always had to be in the middle of everything, checking things out.

Rocky

Rocky colicked in July, 2007. Mum called the vet and he seemed to be better for a short while. It wasn't long after the vet left that he started getting worse. By 2:30 AM he was in such pain that Mum called her son, Scott, and asked him to come and put him down.

Mum said that she didn't want any more horses it was too hard losing them. Besides, she thought she was too old.

Boy am I ever glad she changed her mind.

CHAPTER 10

After Mum told me all about the important horses in her life before me we settled down to a routine in the red barn next to the white house.

For a few weeks that first summer, I had a friend. It was a little bird. I called her Birdy. She would stay on my back until I went into the lean-to. She would fly off my back and wait in the doorway until I went back outside. She would fly back up on my back and off we'd go again!   If Mum took me out on a lead rope to graze on the lawn, Birdy would fly out to where we were. She would stay right by my head and hop along when I moved. It was the first time in my life that I had a bird for a friend. I think she felt safe with me like she knew she was safe being up on my back where a smaller animal couldn't reach her. I liked watching out for her and she was company for me while Mum was at work. I missed her when she left.

One day Mum left the gate open between the barn and garage. I thought I would give Dad a hand by eating the grass so he wouldn't have to mow it. They happened to come out just as I was finishing up. They grabbed a rope and held it so I couldn't go any further. Dad's boat was in the way and I didn't think I had room to turn around. I just kept turning my head to make sure I was backing straight and backed up until I went through the gate. You should have heard Mum say to Dad. "You can't tell me she hasn't been harnessed before. Junie-B, you are so smart, you little darling."

Aw shucks Mum, it was nothing.

It makes me feel good she thinks I'm so smart. She didn't think I was so smart the last time she rode me though. Someone had cut down a bunch of trees right in the middle of the trail. She tried to make me go around. Instead I went right through those downed trees. Mum said, "Junie Beatrix Hawkins, you're going to break both our necks. Go around!"

Relax Mum, I know what I'm doing.

I never missed a step. After we got through it, Mum relaxed and said I had scared the devil out of her. She said that Dew McGregor would have tripped over his own shadow.

I'm sorry Mum. I didn't know.

"From now on, Baby Girl, I'll trust you completely," Mum said.

For the rest of the ride I stepped a little higher, just hearing her say I was better than Dew. It made me feel so good because I knew how much she loved him.

In the fall Mum was cleaning up her vegetable garden. I tried to help by eating the string bean and pea vines and even ate the corn stocks whenever I could reach them under the fence. It was all cleaned up except the big patch of carrots. Mum was waiting for her friend Linda to come because half the carrots were supposed to be hers. I got lucky because during the night a deer broke the fence and guess what? I went in and ate all the tops off before I realized what was just below in the dirt. The next morning Mum happened to look out the window while I was excavating the whole patch. She came on the run and got on her hands and knees and started throwing some over the fence. I was eating as fast as I could.

They were sooooooo. good! Sorry, Linda, I just couldn't help myself.

Once when Mum took me out for a ride I was trotting. Even though she was bouncing a little, it didn't bother me. Most of the time Mum just wanted to walk. She said two old girls should just take it easy and enjoy life in the slow lane. She told me that when she's riding me it's like riding a couch.

When Mum was working cleaning up the pasture or barn, she had a habit of humming or singing. I liked to listen to her even though she said she couldn't carry a tune in a bucket if she had to!

What is a tune and how could anyone carry it in a bucket? It must be hard to do if Mum can't do it. I wonder if it's why no one has asked her to sing in the church choir? Heck Mum, you could even sing a solo if you wanted to, well perhaps not a solo, but you could still sing in the choir.

One cool crisp fall day, Mum explained that hunting season would start the next day. While she was dressing me in my orange hunting costume, she told me that when Dad was dating her and even after they got married, he used to call her "Bullet," after Snuffy Smith's hound dog. He stopped calling her Bullet after he went into the Coast Guard. He said something about how it didn't sound appropriate. I hoped he didn't think she looked like a dog. She told me he called her Bullet because she was loyal and faithful, like the dog. That made more sense.

One day while deer hunting, they jumped a deer. They followed it until the road in the woods divided, Mum went one way and Dad the other. Dad saw the deer heading Mum's way and yelled "Bullet, headed your way." Mum saw it and fired the gun. All of a sudden, they heard a man yelling "don't shoot, don't shoot."

They didn't have any idea there was anyone else in the area. Mum said, "Poor guy, we must have scared the daylights out of him. He probably hid for the rest of the day." Mum said she and Dad laughed all the way home.

I think Mum missed the deer on purpose. She couldn't kill an animal. Way to go, Bullet!

Mum's youngest brother, Jeff, was only seven years old at the time. He liked calling his sister Bullet. He still calls her that sometimes.

CHAPTER 11

Mum's brother, John, came out to see me and I heard Mum tell him that I mean more to her than any other horse she's ever had.

John said, "Are you kidding me, even more than Dew McGregor? Wow, that's incredible! She must be special. She sure is the biggest horse you've ever had."

"Maybe it's because she's had such a rotten life," Mum said." For her to be able to trust any human after all the terrible abuse she has suffered still amazes me. When I first got her, I couldn't touch her head. Now I can hug it."

One day, Mum borrowed Sandy's trailer and took me over to the farm where Black lives so I could have work done on my teeth. As soon as Black saw me get out of the trailer, he whinnied a greeting and ran to the fence. I didn't know that I would see him again and it was so good to catch up. I had missed him and had wondered if he had been as lucky as me. He told me that he was very happy. Sandy and Clarissa loved him very much. I'm so glad. He was a good friend to me.

I wished we could have talked longer, but I needed more work done on my teeth. Jana did the work after the vet tranquilized me. My teeth felt so good then; no more sharp edges. When we left I heard Sandy tell Mum that she would come and get us some weekend and we all could go on a trail ride. I can hardly wait.

That first winter we had lots of snow. Mum always laughed when I rolled. She would say "Are you making snow angels Junie-B?"

Yeah, winter is my favorite time of the year. No bugs!

The next storm was even bigger. Mum had gone out to the pasture while I was eating my grain. The snow was almost up to Mum's hips and she was walking in the path I had made. She turned and started back in just as I started out of the barn. Mum pointed her finger at me and said "Junie Beatrix Hawkins, this path is only wide enough for one of us."

I know, Mum, as I nudged her off the path. Down she went and started making all kinds of snow angels while trying to get up. I turned around and stopped beside her and put my head up as high as I could. I put my lip up in the air and gave her a big smile. She laughed at me as she blamed me for doing that on purpose.

Yeah, I did. After she got up we gave each other a big hug.

The next storm was another big one. When the man plowed Pat's driveway it covered up the fence. I didn't know I walked over the fence until I was in Pat's driveway. Instead of going back the same way, I went down Pat's driveway onto the main road and almost got hit by a trailer truck. That was scary! A man in a pickup truck stopped and tried to catch me. No way was I going to let him catch me. What if he tried to take me away? I ran back in Pat's driveway. The man got into his truck and drove in Mum's yard. I waited to see what would happen. Mum came running out of the house while trying to get her coat on. It was 7 degrees out and the wind was blowing. Mum didn't even take the time to grab a hat or her gloves. She ran into the barn and got a lead rope and started calling to me. I came through the trees, but the fence was in the way. I turned back to to find another way. Mum had to run down her driveway and up the hill to Pat's. The man had blocked the end of Pat's driveway with his pickup truck, so I couldn't   go that way.

Mum was all out of breath when she got to Pat's. I was prancing and snorting, making it very difficult for the man to hang onto my halter. He told Mum that his grandfather had draft horses while he was growing up. Mum said that was probably why he dared to catch me. Mum thanked the man and led me home. She put me in the barn and gave me grain to eat while she went to get more clothes on. When she came back out, she went up and closed the gate going into Pat's pasture for the rest of the winter.

Mum said, "Junie-B, you could have been killed and it's a

wonder I didn't have a heart attack. Please don't ever go near the road again."

I won't Mum, I promise.

One day in early spring I was standing under my favorite pine tree, just thinking about my life. Mum came up and put her arms around my neck and gave me a hug. I put my head over her shoulder and gave her a hug back. She loves it when I do that. She said she thought I looked sad.

Oh no Mum, I'm so glad to be here. I love it here. I'm happier than I've ever been. It's just that I wish I could have always lived here and had my babies here. I could have raised them like a mother should. I would have loved them so much. I know they never had a chance.

Mum said maybe she should find another horse so that I would have a companion and she could invite a friend to ride with us.

It would be nice to have someone to talk to.

I wondered how she would talk Dad into getting another horse. Then I realized that Dad was a pushover, besides he really likes to make Mum happy.

Mum said that when she mentioned it to Dad, he said, "You really aren't serious about getting another horse, are you? How about me buying you a horse trailer so you can take her riding whenever you want." Mum told him that I really needed a companion. Big surprise! Dad caved.

Every Thursday, Mum would get "Uncle Henry's," an advertising magazine, to look for horses for sale. They looked at several, but none of them seemed the right match. Mum did find one ad that sounded good. When she answered the ad and talked to the lady on the phone, the lady said she wanted to free lease her daughter's horse. She asked Mum where she lived. When Mum told her Eddington, she said that it was too far away. She said that her daughter wanted to be able to visit the horse whenever she came home from college. They had owned Freckles, a small Arabian, for many years and were very attached to him. Mum said that she didn't blame them for wanting Freckles closer to home. They kept talking and Mum told her about rescuing Twiggy and bringing her and Dusty back from Puerto Rico. After talking for a while, the lady changed her mind and wanted Mum to come and see Freckles.

The next day Mum and Dad drove to the lady's friend's house to see Freckles. Her friend had another horse and two young girls that liked to ride. Freckles had a heavy coat and didn't look thin. When Mum ran her hands over him, she remarked how thin he was. Mum asked where they kept their hay and the lady pointed to a building. The building was empty. The lady was in tears and told the people that she would be taking Freckles back that day. She was determined to get him back to good health.

What's the problem Mum? You love to take on horses that need you.

Mum said that sometimes the people you think will take the best care of an animal don't. It's in the animal's best interest to follow up and keep checking on them as long as you have a say. It happened to Mum once when she free-leased Dew McGregor. He wasn't getting the best care he deserved and she took him back. Mum said Freckles would be fine as she felt bad for the owner. Mum would have liked to have had him. He was a sweet horse.

It wasn't until May 2009 when Sandy found an ad on the computer and gave it to Mum. Mum was so excited. "Junie-B, I think we have found the perfect horse." She read the ad to me.

"Slightly overweight, underactive, middle-aged mare looking for human companion of same description. I like going for long walks and being brushed. Good with vet, farrier, road safe, and trailers well."

Mum called right away and made arrangements to go see her in southern Maine. She and Dad left that very afternoon. I couldn't wait for them to get home. I was betting on Sandy's ad.

After all, if it weren't for Sandy, I never would have found Mum. Sandy is definitely one of my favorite people!

It was nearly midnight before Mum and Dad got home. I nickered to Mum so she'd come in the barn and tell me what happened. She said, "Junie-B, you have a sister and she'll be here Saturday. Her name is Dixie and she's a chestnut 15.2 hands (a hand is four inches), seventeen-year-old Belgian Quarter horse cross. Her owner even said they'd deliver her."

On Saturday, Mum brushed me until my coat looked like satin. She put me in the big pasture so Dixie and I could get acquainted over the fence. I was so excited when that horse trailer came into the yard. I whinnied a welcome to Dixie. She answered me back. When they let her loose in the small pasture, she came right over to the fence to say hello. We were instant friends, no kicking or biting or anything.

Junie-B and Dixie

Dixie said she was so happy to have a pasture with so much grass. She didn't have a pasture at her other home. She said that she would miss her owners as they loved her and were very good to her. Sandy came over and bought their horse trailer, so everyone was happy.

Mum says I am her baby girl and I will always be her favorite. She loves all 1800 pounds of me. Yes, I have gained 300 pounds since I've been here.

One day I was coming into the barn as Mum was going out with an armload of hay. I guess I think because my head goes through, I have enough room. Well, the door wasn't wide enough for both of us and I squished Mum pretty badly. She said something popped. After a couple of weeks, she got better and it no longer hurt her to laugh or bend over. For that I am thankful. I would never hurt Mum on purpose.

Marie (Mum's best friend) Jamie (Mum's Niece) Rebekah (Mum's Granddaughter) and Kate (Mum's Niece) and me

Dixie and I had a great summer. Chris liked to ride Dixie. Rebekah came for the summer and she and her cousins, Lauren, Kate and Jamie enjoyed riding on Dixie and me. One day when Marie was visiting, she let Jamie, Rebekah, and Kate all get on me at once. I was very careful so nobody would fall off.

Whenever Auntie Linda came out, Mum would let her ride me. She knew I would take good care of her. Mum would ride Dixie.

Mum put two fans in the lean-to and kept them on day and night for the whole summer. Dixie and I would stand in front of them when it was hot or when the bugs were bad. Life was good.

Mum's Grandson Chris on Dixie

*Mum's Granddaughter Rebekah on Dixie,
with Mum's best friend Marie giving her a lesson*

Mum's Grandson Chris on me

Mum's friend Alexis, the first one to ride Dusty

CHAPTER 12

One day in November, when Mum, Dad, and Chris came home from church, Chris asked Mum if she wanted to saddle up. It was cold, windy, and the weather forecast was for sleet and freezing rain. Mum thought, "You have got to be kidding it's freezing out!." Then she thought, "How often will I ever get asked to go riding with my grandson?" Her answer to Chris was, "Sure, let's saddle up."

We were gone for two and a half hours and had so much fun! One of my easy boots came off going up a rocky hill. Mum held Dixie while Chris got off and went to find my boot. He found it but couldn't put it back on. We ended up going down the main road to get home. It started sleeting just before we got home.

When Mum first got me, I had very high withers and she had a hard time finding a saddle to fit me. Several horse people told Mum that at my age the area around my withers would never fill in. Well, guess what? I'm now nice and round and Mum says the 300 pounds I gained went to all the right places. The only downside was that it was hard to keep the saddle from slipping. After two and a half hours, the saddle was quite loose. Mum didn't use the steps to dismount she just swung her leg over. Before she could get her foot out of the stirrup, the saddle and Mum slid down over my side and Mum landed on her rump on the ground.

Oh no, I hope Mum didn't get hurt.

Chris was trying to keep a straight face until Mum started laughing; they both had a hard time to stop laughing while Mum struggled to her feet. Then I saw Mum cross her legs.

Oh, oh, you'd better get into the house Mum before it's too late!

When Mum came back out of the house she said, "I wonder how many people saw that performance?" That led to another story.

This story happened during the ice storm in 1998. John

and Betty Goffin were visiting them and they were supposed to leave for home that morning. They were unable to go as the whole yard was covered with ice and it was raining. Water on top of the ice made it impossible to stand up. Mum waited until late in the morning and knew she had to get out to the barn to feed the horses. It's downhill from the house to the barn so she bent over and hung onto a bucket and slid to the barn! Getting back to the house wasn't as easy.

Dad and John ended up throwing her a rope and reeled her in like a beached whale.

I don't even know what a beached whale is. Must be something that Mum thinks doesn't make her look so good. She looks good to me no matter what she's doing!

Mum always tells me how beautiful I am. I know how bad I looked when she first saw me. It must be true that beauty is in the eyes of the beholder.

After Mum got back in the house, she wondered how many people saw her being reeled in on her stomach. No wonder cars slow down when someone's in the dooryard. This place seems to provide a lot of entertainment. People are always telling Mum she should write a book. Maybe she will someday.

CHAPTER 13

The following spring, I developed an ulcer in my front foot and it took a long time to heal. Then I started to have trouble getting up. Brenda, Mum's friend, moved back from Florida and lived with them then. Brenda is very strong and she would snap a lead rope to my halter and pull as hard as she could to help me up.

Mum called the vet and she came to see me. The first thing she told Mum to do was put me on a diet. My suspensory ligaments in my hind legs were basically shot. The accident that happened when I lived with my abusive master so many years ago was the cause. Nothing could be done as the damage was permanent.

My weight now was just too much. Mum cut way back on my grain, but she let me have all the grass and hay I wanted. It took a while before I finally lost about a hundred pounds and was able to get up easier.

The summer passed. I worried that I was a burden to Mum, even though I knew she loved me with all her heart. Mum took me for walks and spent hours brushing me. She always seemed to know what I was thinking and reassured me over and over I was never going to leave here. I would give her a big hug that always made her smile.

One day while Mum was letting me graze on the lawn, a lady drove in the yard. It sounded as if she hadn't seen Mum in a long time and she asked how Dad was. She had heard that he had a lot of health issues. Mum told her that he was doing fine. "You know Bill, he's tougher than a boiled owl. I've tried to kill him a couple of times."

WHAT, you tried to kill Dad?!! I stopped eating and stepped closer. I didn't want to miss anything.

"Relax Junie-B, it was an accident, I didn't really try to kill him."

The lady had an odd expression on her face and said, "That horse acts like she knows what you just said!"

"Oh, she does. She's my baby girl and we understand each other perfectly. Two hearts, one soul. Isn't that right, Junie-B?"

Yeah. I nodded my head up and down.

Mum, I think you better stop talking. She's going to think you are losing your marbles.

Then Mum told the woman the story.

CHAPTER 14

Dad had a longhaired cat that he had really bonded with. Something like Mum and me. Mum got the cat from a girl who was going to move out of state. The cat's name was Missy, but Dad called her Furball and that's what they called her for the next ten years.

Dad had diabetes and after a couple of years, Furball got diabetes, too. Mum had to give her insulin shots twice a day. Herein lies the problem.

They both took the same kind of insulin. One day Mum got the bottles mixed up and gave Dad Furball's insulin. Dad only used his needles once, but Mum used a needle on Furball several times. That meant the insulin was contaminated.

Furball

The next morning at work she told a friend what she had done. Within minutes it seemed as if the whole hospital knew about it. Everyone kept asking Mum, "How's Bill doing?" Mum would say, "Oh, he's still purring and coughing up hairballs."

The lady asked if she had told Dad what happened. Mum assured her that she had he has a good sense of humor and he loves Furball.

Dad's purring and coughing up hairballs is pretty funny.

He and Mum made a good pair as they seem to find humor in everything. Mum`s always saying, "You might just as well laugh about it as cry about it."

Mum also told the lady she almost drowned him once.

The lady seemed so serious and asked what happened.

I don't think you know my Mum very well. She would never drown Dad on purpose.

Mum told the lady that Dad had sleep apnea, which means he stops breathing when he is sleeping. He has to wear a mask with a hose attached to a machine. It pushes air into his lungs to help him breathe. The machine holds water that keeps the air moist. Mum was filling the tank with water while Dad was lying on the bed with the mask on. She couldn't tell how full the tank was so she picked it up to see better. Once the tank was higher than Dad, the water filled Dad's mask. Dad yanked the mask off and water went everywhere.

Once Dad stopped choking and was apparently ok, Mum said she cracked up. Dad laughed, too, after he asked her if she was trying to drown him.

If I were you, Dad, I'd fill my own tank. Nothing against you, Mum, but it might be safer.

CHAPTER 15

I knew it was hunting season again, because Mum had the orange fleece on my halter. One morning, I was laying in the garden and I had a terrible pain in my belly. When Mum came out to feed me, she called to me and I tried to get up and couldn't. I heard her say "oh, no" as she went into the barn. I knew it scared her when I couldn't get up, so I tried really hard again and managed to stand up. By the time I stood up, Mum was in the pasture. She was relieved to see me standing and called for me to come. The pain was so bad I only took a few steps. Mum came running to see what was wrong. When she saw me shivering, she knew I was in trouble. I was never cold. She kept encouraging me to follow her to the barn. She put a warm blanket on me and went to call the vet. He was on a farm call and said it could be several hours before he could come. Mum gave me a whole tube of medicine and it did help to ease my pain. She took my temperature and it was up. I knew Mum was worried.

Dad had a doctor's appointment and Mum cancelled it. His blood sugar was too high for him to drive. Later, the doctor called and wanted Dad to come in. He still wasn't able to drive so Mum had to take him.

Mum called Scott and asked him to come and stay with me. She called a couple of times to check on me. Scott told Mum that I was standing quietly watching out the window.

Just as Mum and Dad were leaving the doctor's office to come home, the vet called. He asked if Mum still wanted him to come. She said YES! He came shortly after Mum got home. She took my temperature again and it was higher than it was earlier. Dr. Dennis listened to my heart and bowel sounds and watched my breathing. He told Mum that I was a very sick horse. He wanted to put a needle into the bottom of my belly to draw off some fluid. He tried but the needle wasn't long enough. He told Mum he needed to tranquillize me in order to make a small incision in the bottom of my stomach for the needle to reach. He asked her to take me outside. Mum held my head while Dr. Dennis gave me some medicine to make me sleepy. Then he made a small cut in the bottom of my belly and withdrew some fluid. I heard him tell Mum the fluid had food particles in it. That meant my stomach had ruptured.

Dr. Dennis went to get the shot that would end my life. Mum was sobbing and holding me.

It's ok, Mum, please don't cry...
I feel like I'm floating...
the pain is gone...
I love you...

EPILOGUE

By Judy Hawkins

My precious, beautiful Junie-B slipped gently away on November 10th, 2010. I couldn't believe she was gone. I was so thankful Dr. Dennis was able to come when he did. The last thing I wanted was for her to suffer.

She will be missed. Of all the horses I have owned, she was the one who meant the most to me. Maybe it was because she had suffered so much abuse in her life. Everything happens for a reason. God intervened on that fateful day in March in 2008. He knew we needed each other. She did more for me than I did for her, I'm sure. I'm so grateful she chose me. Junie-B taught me a lot and there wasn't a day she didn't make me smile. Standing there I couldn't help but think of the beautiful poem, "The Rainbow Bridge."

The Rainbow Bridge

Just this side of heaven is a place called the Rainbow Bridge. When a horse dies that has been especially close to someone here, that horse goes to the Rainbow Bridge. There are meadows and hills for all our special horses so they can run and play together.

There is plenty of food, water and sunshine and our horses are warm and comfortable. All the horses who had been ill and old are restored to health and vigor. Those who were hurt or maimed are made whole and strong again, just as we remember them in our dreams of days and times gone by.

The horses are happy and content, except for one small thing. They each miss someone very special to them who had to be left behind.

They all run and play together, but the day comes when suddenly one stops and looks into the distance. The bright eyes are intent, the eager body quivers. Suddenly she begins to run from the group, galloping over the green grass her legs carrying her faster and faster.

You have been spotted, and when you and your special horse finally meet, you cling together in joyous reunion, never to be parted again. She'll nuzzle your face; your hands again caress the beloved head, and you look once more into the trusting eyes of your horse, so long gone from your life but never absent from your heart.

Then you cross the Rainbow Bridge together.

Even with the tears still rolling down my face, I smile just thinking about the look of joy on Junie-B's face as she crosses the Rainbow Bridge and sees all her babies who were so cruelly taken from her at birth. You're going to be a wonderful Momma, Junie-B.

Dew McGregor, Tammy, Dusty, Twiggy, and little Rocky will be waiting to greet you, too.

No more pain for any of them. They too will have lots of stories to tell about their adventures with Mum. Hasta la vista, baby girl, until we meet again, and we will.

I told my sons, Scott and John, that when I die, I want some of my ashes put on Junie-B's grave. In 2013, Scott and Judy and John and Stephanie surprised me with a beautiful headstone that says it all. It means the world to me.